FULL FARE

This title is number one in the Frayed Edge Press Street Smart Series

Other titles in the series include:

Down and Out in Paris, with Cat by R.A. Bolo

The Accidental Anarchist by A.R. Melnik

Stealing MacGuffin by Matthew Kastel

Pele's Domain by Albert Tucher

FULL FARE

Jean-Bernard Pouy

Translated by
Carolyn Gates, Jean-Philippe Gury,
and Robert Helms

Frayed Edge Press
Philadelphia, PA

Published by Frayed Edge Press in 2019

Illustrations by Bruce Orr

https://www.frayededgepress.com/

This book is printed on acid-free paper

Publisher's Cataloging-in-Publication Data

Names: Pouy, Jean-Bernard, 1946- author. | Gates, Carolyn, translator. |
Gury, Jean-Philippe, translator. | Helms, Robert, translator.
Title: Full fare / Jean-Bernard Pouy ; translated by Carolyn Gates, Jean-
Philippe Gury, and Robert Helms.
Description: Philadelphia, PA : Frayed Edge Press, 2019. | Series: Street
smart series ; 1 | Originally published in 1994 as "Plein tarif." | Summary:
As the temperature drops, Paris authorities make a plan to prevent deaths
of the homeless: house them in disused train cars on the outskirts of the
city. This unintentionally creates a social and political experiment that
leads to a new form of society -- and causes the police and authorities
to clash with the homeless train dwellers and the anarchists who've come
to support them.
Identifiers: LCCN 2019946794 | ISBN 9781642510096 (pbk.) | ISBN
9781642510126 (ebook)
Subjects: LCSH: Anarchists--Fiction. | Families--Fiction. | Homeless
persons—France—Fiction. | Passenger trains--Fiction. | Paris (France)
-Fiction. | Poor—France—Fiction. | BISAC: FICTION / City Life. |
FICTION / Political.
Classification: LCC PQ2676.O944 F85 2019 | DDC 843 P6--dc23
LC record available at https://lccn.loc.gov/2019946794

FOREWORD

In the United States you have over time forgotten the train, or at least the "mythical" presence of the train.

In Europe, which has obstinately resisted the plane and the car, the train has remained the only means of truly mass transportation, where one can still dream, doze, sleep, chat, flirt, and above all, read. It's a place of calm, and sometimes of rest and happiness. The train has always been a means of transportation of various kinds, including the sensual (remember, Americans, the famous tunnel scene in Hitchcock's *North by Northwest*).

And even if there is a technocratic tendency toward becoming cold, impersonal, expensive, policed, and complicated in actual practice, it remains for the most part a place recognizable by all, a value, a habit, a public service, even if a threatened one. And, for certain people, it still represents the future. Terrorists of all kinds aren't mistaken; they have attacked it for a long time.

Thus, we should render unto the train its power of accommodation: the train as shelter. Try to forget the death trains of the Second World War. The train is a social, political place: a place of mixing and inclusion.

It must also be said that in our privileged societies there is generally enough to provide for the needs of everyone. We only need to decide to do so. Within this movement of possible sharing, the train, of course, also has its place.

It is time to recognize the train as a symbol of freedom.

J.B. Pouy, April 4, 2004

We passed alongside other deserted train cars, lined up head to tail on a garage track.... We were crossing a sort of border. We were going farther than where society wanted to push us.

First, there's the smell. It's a wall of stench, somehow concentrated: a mixture of the foul reek of cold cigarettes, the smell of feet, whiffs of burnt fat, the mildewy funk of cheap wine, and farts blowing at force twelve on the Limburger scale. One hit of it made you want to immediately turn around and go back, made you want to scour out your mucous membranes with Ajax.

But all this could have been just some sort of rite of passage. If you could reach the point where you could mentally plug your nostrils, if you managed to block the work of the olfactory nerve between the nose and the brain, you could go on.

I had just climbed into the train car, as relaxed as an American entering an abandoned cheese cellar. But thanks to a chronic sinus infection, my nasal passages were not exactly sterile and I could stand it.

I had come to visit Uncle Guy. I found him in the second compartment, in the company of a fat woman in a dufflecoat, who snored on the seat with her head leaning against a mutt as filthy as his mistress. It started barking like a hyena as soon as I stopped in the doorway.

"Fuck! Here's my family!" bellowed my uncle. "And they sent the little louse in the vanguard!"

"Hello, Uncle. I thought you hated to travel."

"Shit, it's taken me seventy years to find a train that doesn't budge! It reminds me of the old transit strikes."

"How are you?"

"What do you care?"

I had come to visit Uncle Guy.
I found him in the second compartment...

"Have you got your ticket?" I joked. That gave him a good laugh.

"That's good. You may be a bastard like the rest of them, but at least you're not as stupid."

I was used to this abuse. The insults weren't really about me. Even though Guy bitterly told me to leave him alone on a regular basis, I knew he really loved me. These epithets were really directed at people in his previous life. It was precisely against them that he had built this barrier, as smelly as it was effective.

My uncle is a hobo. That's just how it is. After my aunt's death, from as cutting-edge a cancer as you could ask for, including final moments so painful and horrible that it actually became irrefutable proof of the non-existence of God, he'd been in a depression as deep as 1929. And then, upon returning from a treatment of prescribed rest, he'd dropped everything, sold everything, spent everything, and become a tramp. But not exactly the "saintly" kind. He was a typically Parisian, Place de Vosges section-type tramp. As long as you're bumming around on the street, you might as well choose an historic district; as long as you're crashing under an arch, it might as well be from the 17th—the Century, not the *arrondissement*.

When winter came, the whole family tried to take Uncle back under its wing, trying to assuage the guilty conscience they felt for not having taken such good care of Auntie during her illness. They'd tried to settle him in a warm place, with the secret hope of seeing him abandon this lifestyle, which had cast a purulent shadow over the dignity of the whole clan. He refused, telling all of us to take a hike, and remained out under the stars, even though they were invisible in the city sky.

He had enough dough to survive, Camembert, cheap wine, and whiskey for the holidays; all his junk was stuffed into a disgusting leather bag. His distinguishing mark was his shoes. There was no way he would ever go barefoot in the cold, and his last remaining vanity was that he would never wear slippers split open by the roughness of the asphalt. He was the only beggar walking around in Clarks. He always had great shoes, even if he never washed his feet.

"People put stinky cheese on silver plates, so, fuck it!" he would howl at me.

Whenever I was passing through the Marais district, I would always end up finding him in one of the usual corners of his territory. We would chat for a moment and he'd invariably end up calling me a slave and telling me to go back to my precious studies; his advice was that I should instead use my energies to wreak havoc in the family, the factory, or in society.

I liked him a lot, Uncle Guy. There were people who had generals in their families, or government ministers, but us, we had a tramp.

"You must have thought I'd croaked, huh? Did they pop open a bottle of champagne, those pricks?"

"Not really. Me, I was a bit worried. Them, I don't know."

"Them, they can drop dead."

"They're dead already, you keep saying."

"They can drop dead again."

I had found him in the second compartment of the third coach of the last train. I was relieved because Uncle had disappeared for at least two full weeks and we'd even called the morgue. They indeed had two vagabonds in their drawers, frozen, of course, but they were two younger ones.

I had looked in all the usual homeless shelters until I realized that it could only be here that I would track him down: the homeless train.

"You're cozy here," I said. "It's almost like a Pullman. Or the Orient Express. At least it's warm."

"Forget about it. You wouldn't understand. But I'm happy to see you and I'll introduce you to my pals. It'll be good for your education; a nice change from those turkeys you hang out with—because you're a chickenshit."

Then, very carefully, I sat down on a green vinyl seat and quietly contemplated the fat lady who was still snoring. The dog, on the other hand, had at least shut up. He was looking at me from the corner of his eye. He could tell I wasn't a friend, but I wasn't an enemy, either. Uncle slipped me a piece of Camembert cheese. He seemed to me like a Yaqui sorcerer, handing me my first hallucinogenic mushroom.

"You know, it's terrible," he continued, "of course it's warm here. But all of a sudden, all this chaos. People should come and visit us. The homeless, they're not just penniless guys. They're drunks, too. Only the rot-gut warms you up out there. When the blood boils, the meat doesn't freeze. They're living garbage dumps. The grime keeps them warm the same way. They are sick people. It's incredible how many diseases there are, lying around on the sidewalks. Poor folks, it's sad. It's mean. Every man for himself, since there's nothing to expect from others."

I had to agree, and I had my reasons.

"Yesterday in the Metro," I told him, "I saw a homeless woman, begging. Not too dirty, not too drunk, as you'd say. She was passing between the riders, her little hand cupped in front of her. She seemed to be thinking aloud. She was telling people that, the day before, someone had actually spit in her hand. Well, there was a guy sitting on a jump seat, and he gave her a 200 franc note. She was stunned. She tried to give the money back, saying that it wasn't possible, that he shouldn't. The guy told her that he too was from the North, and that he'd recognized her accent. The woman started crying, holding onto the bar by the door. At the next station, in tears, she said to the guy, "I'm sorry, I have to get off." She sat down on a bench right in front the door and kept crying, all hunched up.

"You see? You see?" Uncle bawled, sure of himself.

I didn't see anything, but I kept my mouth shut. The Camembert was sticking to my teeth. Guy passed me his bottle of red. I didn't even wipe off the mouth.

It had been a month since I tracked down Uncle in this fucking "homeless train," and now I was camping out there almost permanently.

The Empty Pocket Express. The Super Sleaze Special.

It had seemed like a good idea in the beginning.

It came into existence after the first time it dropped below freezing one December night. The entire northern half of France was iced over, and public officials started to have the same original ideas, all over again, as they'd come up with the previous year: opening up the dilapidated Metro stations and First Aid centers; school cafeterias expanded for use by the homeless; gymnasia transformed into overnight shelters—and into a Charlie Chaplin movie. The whole kit and kaboodle, the intense Mother Theresaization of the first days of winter.

But the state-owned French National Railway Company had for once distinguished itself: *"Everything is Possible,"* ran their slogan. This time it wasn't a lie, and a few good ideas had led to one that was nearly ingenious. In the sorting yards between the Masséna station and Ivry, not very far from Paris-Austerlitz, there was a station that had been almost abandoned by travelers since the real trains—the ones that look like Boeings without wings—now leave from Montparnasse. The railway headquarters had had to pull one hundred mismatched cars for not being up-to-date or just too old. Some round-the-clock crews had attached them in a line, ten trains in all, on ten tracks. Other crews, paid for by both the Railway and the Ministry of Public Works, had made haste, so to speak, to connect the cars with electricity (provided *gratis* by the electric company) and water. Some plumbers had linked all of the cars with PVC pipes, with the whole thing running into a septic tank which had been hastily dug at the end of one of the tracks.

So, here were a hundred train cars, packed seat by seat with two thousand homeless people, perfectly housed in a cozy myth. The shitters were at one end of each car, kitchenettes at the other; they had doors that close, heat, easy-to-clean vinyl, curtains for those who prefer darkness, and the incredible illusion of stationary travel. Teams of social workers acted as dispatchers, sending an entire mob into this unique form of government-provided housing. A few people raised their voices in protest against the rounding up and "penning" of this crowd of destitutes, noting that there were certainly some ghastly historical precedents. In the Nazi "death trains," people had traveled for free. Some others were offended by such an ugly thought, and an intense media barrage had the effect of calming the public's guilty conscience a little bit. They praised this new-found comfort, the bodies rescued from the impending ice age, and the generosity of the French

National Railway. From all this emerged a politically correct ad slogan: "Save Our Frozen Tramps!"

Inside the trains, it was a demented microcosm.

The coaches were full, but not overcrowded; there were various groups forming by affinity, there was the stench, the party-shouts, drunken screams, barking animals, and brawls for the conquest of rediscovered love or over the protection of some paltry territory. There was some semblance of order, a little of the civic spirit that had been disappearing from modern life: forming a line at the toilets, for example, the first thing that separates humans from other primates. People took their empty bottles to the trash can; they helped the cripples get up and down from the cars, because without platforms the steps were pretty high. Inside, most of the population was ill, staggering along, desperate. There were wounds, mostly unseen, and a pessimism that sometimes carried infection.

Outside, there were some social activists, people distributing food, and charitable organizations. There were journalists, all believing they could win the Pulitzer Prize, and some film makers, re-making *Viridiana*. And of course there were cops, watching out for trouble and making sure this survival zone didn't become a den of thieves.

It sustained the life of the body, but it was the death of the soul.

"Better be careful with your dogs," a police official said, "you should put them on leashes!"

"Hey, who's the dog here?" a tramp responded. "Where's your leash, pal? If your boss tells you to sit, you sit, right? Well, my mutt's the same way."

"Watch your mouth! I'm not your pal!"

"Run along back to your dog house!"

"You and your dog house. We'll send you back there sooner than you think. You'll see. If you think we're paying taxes just to pamper your gang of freeloaders..."

There were other such terms of endearment. The paupers were cozy, but that was no reason to start liking the dicks.

All of the surroundings were freezing under an ice-blue sky. Viewed from the outside, the camp had a Siberian quality; it was an inner city, but with a Mongolian tendency. One could almost see the horses and yaks grazing outside on the sparse, icy grass growing between the tracks. But friendly steam was escaping from the ten trains, and into the dominant shades of dark green, some new curtains were timidly reappearing, some laundry was trying to dry without crystallizing.

Some taggers and graffiti artists in the area had even repainted the sides of some of the cars, but they were getting bawled out by homeless people with a different aesthetic.

"You little bastards! Go tag the police cars instead of messing up this place!"

"Yeah, go on, call the pigs," came the reply. "What are you protecting? Your suburban house? Your garden- gnomes?"

"Buzz off, zombies, or we'll set the dogs on you!"

"You're the dogs!"

A few local bands wouldn't have minded playing some basic rock 'n' roll there, but the security force let them know that this was not a captive audience, not a zoo filled with endangered and exotic species. And even less was it some discounted version of the Hollywood Bowl.

In short, the poor should be left in peace, especially since the state, via the ever-so-nice French National Railway, had informed the population that all of this would be only a short-term situation. Come spring, as soon as the temperature was no longer synonymous with bronchitis and fatal pneumonia for Joe Homeless, the company would retrieve its equipment, completely bleach and disinfect it, and stow it away for the following year and the next round of cold weather. It was not something permanent. The whole thing was an experiment, and like all experiments, they had to draw some conclusions, put their bigwig sociologists and ethnologists on the job to decide how to do it again, and how to do it better.

In view of the operation's success, some voices, this time many of them sharing the same opinion, had spoken up for maintaining what were then called "the trains of life." These people knew very well that the authorities could not easily discontinue the project for at least one reason: the homeless people and other riff-raff, penned in so far from the downtown area, would no longer make the streets of the capital and the Metro tunnels all messy just when the tourists would arrive *en masse* to see the most beautiful city in the world. Maintaining the trains would mean the end of open-air bathing in the public water fountains; the end of public park benches being used as hotel rooms.

Additionally, since the authorities had them—these rejects, these outcasts—right in front of them, they could finally count them (in order to provide services, they'd say), and watch them (to help keep them safe, they'd say), and manipulate them (to prepare them for re-integration, they'd say).

The theoretical battle was rough. There were a few public demonstrations, but they brought together only a handful of activists. The "fourth world" of urban homelessness always discouraged the ideologues. But in article after article, declaration after declaration, the partisans of train-suppression won the day with their iron-clad motto, which had already been frequently used: *"We must not manage want with indignity."* The problem was not with the ghettoization, but with the integration. These were big words.

"I don't want to be integrated!" Uncle screamed.

What followed were three months of peace. These were strange weeks during which I was very often making the trip between my little room on Rue de Charonne and the train tracks near Masséna Station.

All around this immobile pandemonium, redevelopment activities were going on full bore: the big new national library opened her four gigantic book-like wings of glass and steel, like the thighs of an intellectual courtesan. Masséna and its surroundings were passing from an old-fashioned life into a modern death. The thunderous snores escaping from the train cars hardly covered the roars and crashes of the cement mixers.

I really don't know what was pushing me toward the homeless trains. Without having any ready answers in my mind, I was telling myself that, by helping Uncle, by bringing him smokes and, often, alcohol, I was doing my social duty. It was a bit like some do-gooder who visits prisoners. I went to the slammer once, the visiting room of the local jail, to see a friend. It had been scary. Uncle was right; you have to see it to believe it. You have to really know the situation if you want to judge it. Now I was speaking with the train people, trying to understand what was coming out of their generally wine-soaked minds. I didn't argue, just agreed. Sometimes—rarely—some of them would develop an actual philosophy which was organized, coherent, and vengeful. They saw their fate as a punishment. They flogged themselves frequently for their cowardice and lack of culture. They considered themselves an underclass, and very few of them had the hope, and even less so, the strength to fight with. Rather, they were participating in a long, slow suicide. Among these homeless, many called themselves "terminally unemployed." These were terrible, lucid words.

It was probably the "traditional" tramps who were the most wound up. Among them, there were some who were advocates for the total rejection of any social order. They had lived very different lives, but almost always, there was an underlying resolve, healthy and definitive: "Down with work" and "Death to the pigs." This was what brought them closer to the anarchist activists who had rushed up there and were camping near the site. The color black united them: that of the flag on the one hand, and that of grime on the other.

Since setting foot in this little world, I had felt useful. I could handle a fight. However, most of my time was spent making sure that supplies were arriving. Cheap wine was flowing in rivers, but I also had to convince a few doctors to come and work overtime to provide health care on board. Mostly it was skin problems, and a few ill-treated wounds. There were follow-up treatments for bedsores and psoriasis. I was delighted to be elbow-to-elbow with these bums, these romantic libertarians who my family had made me swear never to hang out with nor ever approach. They had convinced me by daily proselytizing and soft-core brainwashing that entropy and chaos were barbarism, that the future lay in Social Democracy, and that everything else is just hard drugs.

Uncle had little by little introduced me to his buddies and pointed out his enemies. His paranoia had chosen some who were very obvious, such as the ones who wanted to take his shoes. He showed me around the place. The homeless, now that they had homes, were starting to decorate their compartments, trying to lighten the place up with some recycled junk, as though they wanted to perfume over the atmosphere of filth and abandonment. We were far from a basic IKEA store, but one couldn't help being surprised by the number of knick-knacks they'd already accumulated. It hadn't occurred to them to tidy the place up, and they had not yet decided to form a neighborhood association, but it didn't matter. They weren't just passive, which was grist for the mill for those who advocated for a second chance for the destitute. Suddenly it became a vast wasteland of metal, a shanty-town on wheels, described by the authorities as a regular petri dish, a shameful canker on a district that served as home for the world's most beautiful library; it had become a danger zone. Some people spoke of cholera. Others spoke of it as an illegal psychiatric hospital; still others, as a hospice for dying alcoholics. Among the more radical, it was called a concentration camp.

It was filthy, this is true. But it was also a lot of fun! The idea that it would all come to an end was just intolerable.

The nice weather returned in the shape of a wandering high-pressure system, ahead of its summer schedule. The social workers tried, at first gently, to evict the stationary travelers by using persuasion and dangling various carrots in front of them. With the exception of a few long-time tramps who returned without balking to their old haunts on the streets (the haughty solitude in which these flowers will bloom at all costs), most of "the relocated," against all expectations, formed an unmovable block. It was out of the question that this railroad squat, given to them with one hand, could be taken away by the other. Below the surface some fights

Finally, on the evening of March twenty-second, the henchmen took a serious beating during an encounter with some eager young anarchists who had rushed over to provide security for the train-dwellers.

simmered, there was some squabbling of striking rudeness, and there were even some actual distress calls. One guy died of natural causes, his liver scratching to get out; two others had to be hospitalized as emergency cases. But that was the worst of it.

The numerous dogs accompanying these shaggy paupers had bitten a few shins and were barking as loudly as those Dobermans guarding the small homes of their owners, behind the apartment towers a bit farther away. The press got involved, and viewed from, say Limoges, the scene looked almost Somalian. The henchmen for the Railway (who had been given a rude nickname by the anarchist paper *Liberatión*, meaning "five out of nine are fascists") manhandled a few people and indulged in a few brutalities. Because of this predictable malfeasance, they got called vigilantes, Vichy cops, and collaborators. Finally, on the evening of March twenty-second, the henchmen took a serious beating during an encounter with some eager young anarchists who had rushed over to provide security for the train-dwellers.

Nobody had really planned that. The red squads were not what they used to be, being too busy infiltrating the Trotskyists, who in turn were infiltrating everybody, so they had not seen the sudden mobilization of the young anarchists, who had just been waiting for this sort of chance to play cops and robbers: the Austerlitz sorting-yard as Parisian battlefield.

The whole affair became bluntly ideological, and suddenly small groups of every kind turned up, all at once, finding their second wind. But the anarchist group, snickering, was more than happy to show the suddenly re-appearing Leninists that they were armed to the teeth with axe handles, slingshots, and Molotov cocktails. They were a Black Revolutionary Guard for the hungry, consciously committed to defend the trains and to not re-live Kronstadt or Barcelona. The closet-commies were accused of train-hopping (hahaha), but they contented themselves with circulating leaflets and petitions, and timidly attempting to lure new recruits. The political big shots didn't even bother to show up. The Right eats at Maxim's, not the soup kitchen; the Left eats caviar, not Campbell's Pork & Beans. The "fourth world" is just too "fifth of Night Train" for them.

Everyone in this weird little world coexisted. Inside, in the cars, a complex humanity had found its niche. Outside, the political and social activists were bent on protecting what they considered to be a victory in the class war.

During that time, members of Parliament from every party made strong, dramatic speeches when the Railway had asked, with a heavy heart, that the Minister of the Interior help them clear the flea-bags out. And they had to act quickly: in the field, their opponents were rapidly reinforcing and getting organized. They had to avoid the recurrence of scandalous episodes like when they forcibly evacuated Berber immigrants from the Sonacotra hostels: the burnoose against the bulldozer. It wasn't good for the image of France, the land of welcome, a nation trying to fight against discrimination, a society reputedly rich and responsible. The high-ranking Railway administrator who first had the idea for the "trains of life" (once seen as generous but now seen as cumbersome and almost unmanageable) had been transferred to Marseille. He had his work cut out for him down there.

I had never seen Uncle like this before. He was almost enjoying a social life again. He was becoming less isolated, having met people like himself, something he didn't think was possible anymore. However, inside this paradoxical village, some forms of discrimination had started to appear. The unemployed and homeless had slowly created an internal selection process, first by screaming matches, then by smacks upside the head. They thought of themselves as being on a sinking ship, but not voluntarily. They managed to slowly eliminate from the cars anyone who didn't look like them.

At the end of March, there was a territorial partition, not very different, I have to admit, from what is seen anywhere else. Uncle, and people like him, the old-fashioned tramps, the stinkiest and loudest ones, the sickest also, the ones who knew almost genetically how to avoid rides in the squad cars, had regrouped in the last train, the one at the back, the one least exposed to view, as if the ones who had put them there wanted to give the world a good impression of their village. Even if geraniums were conspicuously absent from the windows, there was no way you could leave the dirtiest people on full display. It was a question of appearances.

There were two train cars where the people of color had wound up, by no accident, even if the others were saying that it was they who had seceded. The leftists had tried to make the train inhabitants respect the diversity, the integration, the mingling of races, but they broke their own morale in the attempt. It was a ghetto inside a ghetto, a tale within a tale.

Some young runaways had tried to find lodging and meals in the more respectable cars, but they were thrown out. They were told, "Go swipe what's available from your bourgeois parents and redistribute all of it here." A crypto-commie had remarked that this was a class reaction of good omen.

Then the neo-fascists conducted a raid one night. These cretins had succeeded in making a "holy alliance" between themselves, but they only succeeded in bringing everyone on the trains back together as one. The brawl had been quick and brutal; the men on the train had not held their ground, but the dogs quickly made the difference. The distinctive green hunting jackets of the fascists were left in red shreds.

The government couldn't take it anymore. France couldn't brag about having a little Bogotá. It was jarring; it had become dangerous, out of control. The lack of security was on everyone's lips. Only drugs were missing from this confluence of evil deeds, probably because they were too expensive. The homeless train was becoming a more and more unbearable provocation. But still everything remained more or less on the level of "big words and little sorrows."

On April 2nd, there was a death. It had been a quarrel, a squabble over a seat or a stolen bottle, we will never know for sure; in the end, it was simply a story of drunkenness and misfortune. Knives had been drawn and a guy was stabbed to death. Before the paramedics could arrive, the green vinyl seat cover had changed color. The ambulance and the cops arrived later, but everything had been settled. The murderer didn't even hide himself, but was sleeping it off, stretched out in the aisle, his head resting against some empty beer cans. The TV channels, like buzzing shit-flies, followed the cops to the stench, looking for the best turd to film.

Among the anarchist comrades, we knew this was the signal of the end. The media finally had enough bad news to make the viewers sick, to assuage any remaining guilty feelings, and to prepare the ground for what would come next. Since everything had gotten out of control here, in this little Rwandan slum ruled by senseless death, some of course unpleasant but now necessary measures were in order. From now on it was a question of prevention. The time of arrival was announced. The train had never started, but the end of the line was now appearing on the horizon.

We were as jumpy as fleas. At last, we'd be able to fight, to show them what we're made of, to test ourselves in the field of political strategy. We'd whack the good old axe handle on the right helmet. It would not be the "great night" of our ancestors, but it would be a little evening very much appreciated.

The riot squad appeared two days later at 6 a.m., when our dear Babylon was still asleep. The dogs howled with one voice, but they could not cover up the snoring coming from the cars. The poor panicked animals quickly took flight from the tear gas, which clouded the rising dawn. There were not many Trotskyists on duty that day and, even if they showed undeniable courage in trying to block all the doors, they didn't understand the tactics of the forces of order, which were more clever than usual. They didn't launch a frontal attack on the entrenched but dazed camp. Instead, they savaged only the first car of the first train without going further, without going into the whole train to drag out its occupants with iron fists.

We quickly understood why—an engine was coming.

It was an old one, my Uncle told me, but it was one of those which had a long time ago broken the speed record of over 200 miles per hour. I was rediscovering, little by little, my uncle's old passions, each one more surprising than the other. I had realized, for example, that he was passionately interested in history, especially with facts, and that his favorite period was the beginning of the 17th century; that explained why he always used to hang out around the Place des Vosges historic district.

The huge engine brutally slammed into the train, destroying all the sewer pipes and bursting the water lines.

There were some sparks, the lights went off, and some of the pipes dumped out their contents. Inside the train, there was a lot of fierce yelling: the Holler Express. Then, protected by triple ranks of black-helmeted police with shields, some railway workers came and attached the engine to the train. It started squealing, pulling away the ten cars behind it at low speed. A few people jumped from the moving train, falling into the stinking mud and the geysers of running water, but most of the occupants, screaming obscenities and insults out the windows, were dragged along with the train out of the sorting yard.

In the near-silence due to astonishment and surprise, the newly-besieged watched the departure of this ghostly train, creaking along in the early morning light, this Breugel painting on wheels, until it disappeared at the end of the tracks.

And then the fighting started up again at pace. The riot squad retreated in good order, under a rain of various projectiles, and after a ten-minute break they attacked the first car of the next train, because another older model engine was approaching at low speed.

"They could have at least sent us a classier engine, so we could travel in style!" Uncle laughed.

Some people tried to lay down on the tracks but were cleared off by the law, feet first.

Three frenzied guys reached us from the outside, having snuck into the yard by going around by the huge waste incinerator. They told us that the whole neighborhood had been sealed off, from Austerlitz to Ivry, and that we could only count on our own meager forces. Reinforcements would not be coming; waiting for the cavalry was not an option. Our eyes were already red, but bright. Bandanas concealed faces, cases of Molotov cocktails appeared as though by magic, and different tactics were discussed and adopted. The anarchists regrouped in and around the last two trains, thinking that the cops would probably attack them from all sides. The rest of the troops dispersed with the objective of delaying the mopping-up of the trains as much as possible, until the friends, concerned parties, comrades, and maybe even the Parisian populace intervened, raising an enormous demonstration, joining hands and defending the wretched of the rails.

Uncle was ecstatic. It reminded him of the revolutionary activities of '68, he said.

"Oh, right. Like you were there in 1968? At forty years old?" I shot back at him, sure that I could learn some things by pushing him onto this slippery ground. Back then he had been the manager of an insurance company, so I could hardly imagine him manning the barricades.

"You weren't even born, you little squirt, so what would *you* know?"

"My father never told me about this."

"*That* moron? All *he* did in '68 was debate at the Odeon. For him to have been there and to have put out his bullshit gives him the right to say he took part in the revolution. Myself, I didn't participate in the revolution. I didn't know a thing about the revolution. All I know is that on the 24th, I was on the street in my business suit."

"No kidding..."

"Yep! Just wear a tie for thirty years, and you'll find out that you don't want to wash your feet again either. I didn't know what to do. All these young people were giving me funny looks. Maybe they thought I was an undercover cop. In any case, I told myself, 'I have to leave my mark; I

"...there was some construction work: a heap of rubble with fences and a backhoe. So, I climbed into the backhoe and started it up. They're no harder to drive than a car, those things."

have to leave my signature.' At the corner of Boulevard du Maine and the Rue Froidevaux there was some construction work: a heap
of rubble with fences and a backhoe. So, I climbed into the backhoe and started it up. They're no harder to drive than a car, those things. It took me fifteen minutes to flatten one of those disgusting public urinals built up against a wall. After that, I left. Everybody was laughing. I came back a month later. The smashed urinal was still there, like some sort of iron sandwich. But, hey, at least my signature had been there for a month!"

Uncle was right: I didn't know what to say.

Then the trench warfare began, train after train, with incessant victories for the reactionary forces of order. The always-well-to-do were defeating the newly-poor, skirmish after skirmish, ambush after ambush, charge after charge. The riot squad was taking a beating, losing shitloads of helmets, but it still advanced, inevitably. Gasoline bottles exploded in their faces, and they answered this with tear-gas grenades, fired point-blank. The paupers dropped to their bellies in the train compartments and aisles, few among them taking part in the fight, leaving the struggle mostly to the outside combatants. In the corridors, a few of them did take part in the fight. Some, sensing deep inside that they had nothing to lose, charged straight ahead and hurled themselves, screaming, into the big, hairy arms of the forces of order. The most energetic of the combatants were dragged away, clubbed, and thrown into trucks, to be taken away for another beating elsewhere. We learned over the radio, thanks to the two or three squawk-boxes that were still crackling away, that all around the battlefield, everything was calm.

No demonstrations were on the horizon. No journalists had been invited to the party, so they were making do from the windows of surrounding apartments, to follow the carnage at a distance. One journalist saw the battle from so far away that everything he said was bullshit, talking about "hundreds of injured," "the war in Paris," and "Sarajevo at our gates." Another more serious guy managed to get closer to the theater of operations, but he was severely trounced.

"The Press is in danger!" he screamed. "Free speech is being murdered!" But we were alone, as on a stage, with very few spectators. It was a clean-handed operation.

On the other hand, our freedom of speech had not yet been murdered. Insults, filthy names, and other rhetorical devices poured down like rain. I learned a lot of new words. The tramps had one hell of a vocabulary, and they tried it all out in a coughing, spitting barrage. I didn't know that a cop could be fucked up in so many different ways.

We also learned that the trains conquered by the Law and the State were being taken a bit farther away, between Vitry and Choisy, and that the passengers were being handed over to the regular cops there, who in turn brought them to Nanterre, where there was an infamous homeless "shelter." Those who were willing to clear out on their own were set free without too much violence. This was the carrot and the stick, the on-going story of life.

As a result, many of our homeless "protégés" began to exhibit some reluctance. They wanted to surrender. They were scared. Since they knew they'd be set free only a little farther down the line, they preferred to leave right now, rather than going through another hell. Some of them even started to insult us, saying that it was all our fault, that they didn't want anything other than to be left alone, and that little fools like us with our big words weren't going to tell them what to do. Many avoided the persuasive guardianship of the anarchists and left, coughing away. For them, cheap wine in some other place would still be cheap wine.

Uncle himself was holding on just fine. He was having fun, feeling like a kid again, rediscovering his youth: Ah, '36': the demonstrations in espadrilles, the shoulder-bags full of nuts and bolts, the flatfoots who high-tailed it out of there. Ah, '68: the trees felled along the boulevards, and the enormous, flooded hole at the intersection of Boulevards Sainte-Germain and Saint-Michel. In our train—that of the smelly bums— there was a wonderful ambiance, a death-to-the-pigs mood after the hasty withdrawal of the least faithful and the most sickly. Wine is wine, and it makes you warm when you piss it. Some of them had started the battle by hitting the bottle, and the events must have looked to them like the unreal decor of a nightmare, or a party that ends in a fight. Others were angry at the whole world: No mercy. Liberty or death. Fuck those assholes. No gods, no masters. Anarchy rules. Jail the rich and send the teachers to the beach.

It was a glorious day for everyone, a redemption. Silent Night, Drunken Night. We'll probably be the last ones to fall, but we'll keep on fighting till the end; until death; until we quench our thirst.

Time was marked by the waves of attack. It was all happening pretty quickly, not taking them more than fifteen minutes per train. Needless to say, the homeless were not crack troops. Drunk, sick, blinded by the tear gas, drained of strength, they were getting picked off, one by one, just like in 1914. The young leftists learned quickly how to respond, but they were too few in number and they were hampered in their movements by the haphazard and disorderly comings-and-goings of the panicked homeless. The riot squad was throwing them into paddy wagons left and right. Some of the cops had even discarded their shields—too cumbersome—and were clearing out the areas around the cars with billy clubs. They even ventured to do some sorting: the younger ones were herded to one side and thrown into trucks, bound for jail; the older ones were pushed back into the trains by force.

The trains started up with squealing noises, but they gradually became less wild and vocal. The last one we saw leaving had a downright shameful silence to it.

"Destination, Auschwitz," Uncle mumbled through his rotted teeth. "These Nazis won't get me."

By morning's end, eight of the trains had been cleared out, and the terrain had become a total wasteland: a mixture of rails, mud, shit, and garbage. It was not a very cheerful sight, especially under the thick clouds of teargas. Within a few hours, we had gone from Bruegel to Hieronymous Bosch. Hundreds of flashing lights on the cop cars and ambulances were piercing the fog, tracing the almost monolithic silhouette of the riot squad and gendarmes' army, withdrawn for a while before the attack on the ninth train.

I myself was excited, eyes red, exhausted by incessant trips back and forth, trying to persuade the wine-sodden wrecks of humanity to organize themselves for the final clash. Our car was finally ready—it was a real mobilization. Some were laying down under the seats. The doors were blocked by miniature barricades made of stacked objects. Each window was manned by the same number of warriors. The supply of projectiles had been distributed.

But a quarrel had divided the defenders of our castle. Some had suggested that we detach all the cars. That way the invaders would have to do battle at least ten times, and the engine would be able to take away only one car at a time. Others thought the fight would continue in another place, with lower odds, and that we should all stick together. Negotiations took place, and we ended up dividing the train in two. There would have to be two battles instead of one for the attackers, and each train of five cars would still be an army on the march.

The battle for the ninth train was really Dantesque. I was able to see up close that, aided by fatigue and high stress, the violence was becoming very real. The combatants were carried away, often covered in blood, by riot police who had become pit-bulls without leashes. The last organized leftists lost their bet in a gallant manner. They knocked out some members of the enemy forces with the sheer energy of their desperation. All this happened right in front of our eyes. The tramps on my train were terrorized: they almost weren't shouting anymore. They stood there with arms dangling and wild hair, and started to drink again, in order to forget. It was like they were waiting for death.

I was, too. I was living with a bizarre sensation of inevitability. We were definitely going to have our faces smashed in. And this certain fact, instead of scaring me, actually gave me extraordinary strength and energy. I'd never felt like that before. There were no more questions to ask ourselves; we knew we had already lost. But this somehow prevented the anguish, suppressed the fear of physical pain. I thought about all those stories of hopeless battles, such as Camarone or the Alamo, about all those cornered guys who no longer seemed to fear anything. It was as though certain defeat was giving birth to invincibility and a kind of courage. In my street fights I had learned that only the first blow is painful, and after that you don't feel anything. You defend yourself, that's all.

When the ninth train started moving, we saw that many members of the forces of order were on board, blocking the doors. The ride was going to be rough. Some guys escaped from our car through the windows and lurched off, absolutely refusing to face this kind of conclusion. As for myself, I was starting to tremble, unable to stop. Our turn had arrived. It was like being at the dentist's office. As long as there were three people ahead of you, it's OK, but after that it's scary, and you find yourself continually watching the door. I finally realized that I'd felt like running off myself for a long time, that there was nothing to do here but get one's face smashed in or to get shipped off, as if this were a fucking death-train, and wait for the big wash-down a half a mile away. But acting on this idea was becoming impossible. A fight without any hope of victory is no longer a fight: it's suicide. The tramps were moaning, and I saw one crying. Only a few loud ones were rediscovering their youth, with Uncle in the lead. They joined the dozen or so anarchists there defending the train, wild and excited like birds of prey. But there were not enough of us anymore. The police fury was about to sweep us away.

The anarchist next to me seemed to read my mind. He was a tall fellow with a romantic, disabused attitude, but not hiding the tough, complicated tattoos covering his forearms. He was tearing his clothes apart on purpose, rubbing them on the ground to make them filthy, and smearing his face with dirt.

"Don't fall apart," he told me, "If you split now, if you surrender, they'll have time to see who you are, where you come from. They'll have all the time they need to get you. In the heat of the battle, you can blend in. But it's really up to you to decide. Personally, I just *can't* get nabbed. I've been a draft dodger for four years now, and I walked myself right into this stupid trap. I'm going to fight, but at the last moment I'm going to try to get rounded up with the tramps. It may work. I have to believe it will work. Otherwise, I know I'll soon enough find myself serving in a disciplinary unit in Bosnia.

"But—there's only volunteers over there..." I objected.

"You—you believe everything they tell you?" He looked at me as if I was a young novice from a convent. "As soon as things start getting hot, play dead, as if you're unconscious. That way they'll beat you a little less violently. With a little luck you'll get an ambulance ride. It's always better than the paddy wagon."

This draft-dodger was bugging me with his veteran's advice, but at the same time I had to admit that I admired his courage. I suddenly realized that there were plenty of people, roughly my age, who were living very different lives from mine—more thrilling, dangerous, unpredictable—and all this was happening right here in our beautiful society, apparently so tranquil and comfortable.

We watched in stiff silence as the riot squad withdrew to recuperate, to regain some strength, to reorganize themselves, and to reload their guns and weapons. I thought about all those movies that had the same cliché scenes: entrenched before the assault, behind the wagons, before the Apaches arrive, in the belly of a plane before the big jump, with all those idiotic dialogues that everyone knows by heart:

"If you manage to survive, go find my wife, and tell her that I died bravely..."

"If I get out of here somehow, I'll spend a week at a classy hotel, down on the Riviera..."

All of those stupid lines! And the photo of the child that the hero looks at tearfully, the love letter that he dreamily smells. Whatever. In short: There was an incredible tension in the air—like before an injection of sodium pentothal, before utter agony, yeah.

It had been a while since my uncle was by my side. He'd been hanging out with the little group of four or five anarchists who acted, more or less, as the train conductors. They were debating in low tones; one could have called it a council of Sioux elders before the buffalo hunt. I was wondering what they could be saying, or what they might be cooking up. My uncle was in high spirits, not at all worried, and he nodded his head often and started laughing, a bit hysterically. I was thinking what a catastrophe it was that I couldn't tell all this to the family. They would never believe me. Maybe my uncle had been in Diên Biên Phu. You never could tell with him. He was no doubt sharing his own experience as a veteran. Yeah, right; he was probably telling them the public urinal story.

Then, almost transfigured by the importance of having a secret mission, he rigged up a sort of white flag using a scrap of an undershirt, stuck it on a stick, and rushed outside. My uncle was going to sacrifice himself!

I tried to stop him, shouting like a madman: "Come back, Uncle! They're gonna kill you!"

He dodged back through the mud, zig-zagging between the jets of water spilling from the broken pipes, came up to the window where I was, and advised me, with grandiloquence, to observe the lesson of courage I would later be able to report to our flabbergasted family, that family of cowards and living-dead bourgeois.

"And you'll tell them, 'That was a brave man!'"

Then he began to laugh. Even on the edge of tragedy, he had an air of being surprisingly sure of himself. I, however, was ill at ease. Nothing made sense anymore. The tramp of the family had been transformed into a herald. Or into a hero—who knew?

He advanced through the devastated field, stepping over the rails and debris with difficulty. He was going, all alone, towards that pack of black dogs, the uniformed police, who were waiting for him further on, standing around their trucks. I headed to the end of our train car, to the group of anarchists he'd been speaking with. I wanted to find out what their secret meetings had been about, to understand this family sacrifice.

It was quickly made known to me, and I was floored by the naïveté of the thing. My uncle, he was going to parley. He was going to say that we would give ourselves up, but that beforehand, he wanted an eminent member of the French National Railway, accompanied by a representative of the Police Headquarters, to come and see the state of the people that the police were planning to attack, as if they were all potential Mesrines, the infamous "Robin Hood of the Paris streets." They needed to simply see the sickness, the fear, and the fatigue, and realize what was going on. That's all. To see. To know. And afterwards, we would let ourselves be transported away to that other dispatch area, farther away, but with those two VIPs as guarantees. All of this was cooked up as a way to avoid unnecessary violence.

Of course, the whole idea was completely insane. It was obvious that he was going to get clobbered and thrown in the police van, and that would make one less on our side. The cops had not beat the hell out of nine trains full of people in order to make peace with the tenth. They wanted to win ten

It was then that I saw the weapons. Two guys had guns, one of which was all shiny and nickel-plated.

to nothing, and I didn't see any way that they would let us score at the last minute.

I even thought for a moment that my uncle had found the right plan for escape from the massacre, that he was playing a quiet little treason and that he was utilizing the same methods of escape that he had always used with his own family. Bum for a day, bum forever.

But everyone left me alone to my thoughts, and those who were not yet paralyzed by the cheap wine began to speculate. The cops had had too many casualties. This would be a convenient exit door for them as well. If they attacked again, their image would become too deplorable, now, in the eyes of instantly informed mass opinion. The battle had lasted three hours. They owed it to themselves to accept this opportunity, to show that they were not just acting like starving wild beasts maintaining public order, but that they were also clever negotiators. Humanitarians. Intellectuals, almost.

In any case, the anarchists seemed to believe it. The situation in the car was tense, but cheerful, with the Draft Dodger, the Chief Desperado, in command. But I sensed there was a problem somewhere. I worried that they had sacrificed my uncle in their romantic fury for their lost cause. No, they really had a confident air. One of them had even said that this guy, my uncle, was brilliant and that this would be a great day for the cause.

It was then that I saw the weapons. Two guys had guns, one of which was all shiny and nickel-plated. They hid them behind their backs, thrust into the belts of their jeans, under their jackets.

This—this changed the tune for me. The fear that was roiling my stomach was suddenly no longer shameful, there was a reason for it. These bastards were going to put the lives of numerous people in danger for a chance to play out their little war. Weapons. I just couldn't believe it. Reality hit me hard. I had learned that in big demonstrations, there was always one line that was never to be crossed: that of having firearms. It was this line that avoided, for quite some time, many casualties in France. Now, everything was changing, switching into high gear. I decided that if these jerks wanted to get shot at, it would be without me.

I rushed immediately to the middle of the train, fleeing the front line, but I couldn't go farther than the fifth train car. After that, it was the other half of the train, the other fortress. Maybe it was loaded with bazookas. Or rocket launchers. I huddled on a seat. Outside, everything was grey, almost white with smoke and tear gas, like the end in *Gordan Pym*.

Everything was relatively quiet. There were a few sirens in the distance; some barking, some shouting. The sound of water; some creaking. The clatter of the commuter trains, passing nearby. A radio in one of the compartments. There was still no demonstration coming to our rescue, but some slum kids had started torching cars near Bercy. A few store windows had also been smashed, but the forces of order were on top of it. It was nothing but isolated incidents. And there was monstrous commentary on our "village": one of filth and lice, alcoholism and vermin, vague testimonials about the homeless being happy to be free of it. The journalists didn't hold back on the jargon: "The dispatch of horror." "The trains of shame." And also, Abbé Pierre, the activist priest, was requesting an emergency audience with the President.

Twenty minutes later, along with everyone else whose eyes searched the fog, I saw my uncle come back to the train—

staggering, but still brandishing his ridiculous flag, which he was using more like a prod. Indeed, in front of him, two more shadows were advancing towards us. My uncle had succeeded: two officials were coming to visit.

I thought again of the guns and began to tremble, sick to my stomach. They weren't going to shoot them, I told myself. It was impossible. I forced myself to head back up the train cars, stepping over all those silent and resigned bodies. Several tramps had sunk into comatose sleep. No doubt they wouldn't even remember their last battle.

I arrived too late to witness the reception. The first thing I saw was the two guys in raincoats and suits, tied up with ropes, their wrists attached to a window bar, looking bewildered and pale. And then the two anarchists with guns in their hands. My uncle was dancing around, in seventh heaven.

"We won! You lost! Nyaah-nyaa-na-nyaaah-nyaaaaah!"

"Guy, fucking hell! Explain this to me!"

"Napoleon was an amateur compared to us, I tell you!"

"What's going on, Uncle?"

"What's happening is that we're going on vacation, to the sea!"

As soon as the railway official and the police chief had boarded the first train car, the welcoming committee had acted. Voilà, they were all tied up. Then the anarchists had chosen one of the tramps who was in the worst state, gave him a letter and sent him out towards the forces of order. In this letter were "our" conditions, as set forth by the occupants of the "Makhno" train, taking the name of the Ukranian anarchist leader who had raised an army and resisted the incursions of both the White and Red armies during the Russian Revolution. Henceforth, the Makhnos were holding hostage two servants of Power and Capital. They wanted a locomotive. They wanted open rails all the way to Marseille. There, by the time they reached the sea and the end of the line, all France would know about their just cause and then they would surrender.

If not, the two civil servants would be shot.

The two anarchists fired three gunshots into the air as soon as they were sure that their letter of demands had arrived at its destination.

The two tied-up big shots were terrified. There was the smell, the pandemonium, and also the fear.

We waited. Outside, there was silence. A few sirens wailed, farther away.

Inside the train, there was chronic coughing, throat-clearing, and drunken mumbling.

My uncle was sitting on the floor. He was back on the bottle.

"Let's celebrate! I've never had so much fun. They didn't want to come, these bastards. But the TV people were there, I saw the cameras. So, I started bawling. Man, that settled it! These two guys followed me straight away."

"What the hell is this stuff about Marseille?"

"You can send a postcard to my fucking brother!"

"I don't know if you realize, Uncle, but we're at Austerlitz Station! Getting to Marseille is going to be a bit complicated! That's the Bordeaux line. Or through Toulouse."

"We'll go by Béziers!"

"But I don't want to go to Marseille!"

"You fucking idiot, we're not going to Marseille! Marseille? What the hell would I do in Marseille? You're not getting it! If this trick works, in one hour we'll stop the train in the middle of the countryside, and we'll jump out, scatter, and disappear. No one sees or knows anything. Made in the shade!"

I was stunned. They thought they were in the Three Musketeers.

"But these tramps won't be able to go thirty feet in the countryside! There's no one here who could climb over the barbed wire fences."

"Stop whining, damn it. You're not being forced to come along. You're not my babysitter. Go back and join your tight-ass family. Tell them I've moved south. Hey, tell 'em I've become a Green, that's what you should tell 'em."

"Here comes the engine!" shouted one of the lookouts in the front of the train.

We rushed up front in order to be able to see, at crawl speed, an old, bright green engine piercing the haze little by little. Farther away, some shadowy riot squad troops approached, keeping a respectful distance. It seemed like the authorities had accepted the deal. They must have thought of some other way to arrest us. And besides, holding a police chief meant something. And a police chief with a pistol to his head, that was a first.

The engine bumped into the train gently, but everything cut out immediately. There was no more juice, the water pipes were torn out and the PVC toilet hook-ups creaked eerily. A powerful odor of human waste succeeded in imposing itself over the already strong general stench. A guy in blue work overalls came and attached the engine to the first car and ran off, following in the footsteps of the engine conductor who was running away, skirting the rails.

The Draft Dodger and one of his buddies untied the railway official and pushed him out, a gun barrel stuck against his jaw, in full view of everyone. They clambered into the engine. My uncle explained to me that all these train-bosses were able to drive a train. The police chief tried to tell us to cut our losses before things got any more serious, that all this was a big mistake, but my uncle threatened him, saying that if he didn't shut up he would stuff his bottle of cheap wine down his throat and then gag him with his own socks. The guy blanched, ready to faint.

We waited another long moment.

My uncle, on the foot-rail, hanging on to the iron handrails, was looking off into the distance. The signal was still red. Everyone was tense. No one quite believed it yet. It all seemed incredibly insane.

"It's green!" shouted my uncle. "They've opened the track! We've won!"

A blast of the whistle, coming from the locomotive, replied.

The train started its engine. Everyone started cheering.

At slow speed, the five train cars passed in front of the riot squad, who came nearer to see their prey escaping. There was a volley of insults, with unexpected variations, shot out from all the lowered windows. Stylish exercise routines based on giving the finger were spontaneously invented. There was intense mocking laughter, and the drunken feeling of certain victory.

I relaxed a little bit. I couldn't see any viable outcome to this ghostly trip, but we had escaped a police beating, so we could breathe a sigh of relief.

We passed Choisy-le-Roi at slow speed.

It was a beautiful, sunny day and a little fresh breeze came in through the open windows. Exhausted and worn out by the fighting and the tension, many guys were already asleep, often on the floor, in the middle of empty beer cans and the residue of the siege. In certain compartments there was loud snoring, despite the noise coming from outside, despite the flapping curtains. We passed alongside other deserted train cars, lined up head to tail on a garage track. Two police cars stood guard. We shouted, vengeful fists raised, we laughed, everyone was hysterical. We were crossing a sort of border. We were going farther than where society had wanted to push us. The victory was complete. It was a grand slam, a bloodbath.

"But they will block the track at some point," I said to my uncle. "At a switch. We won't be able to go on. It'll be someplace quiet, far from everything, where they can massacre us without any journalists present."

"Stop worrying, there's no risk of that," he replied. "Don't forget two things: we have two hostages, and, in the locomotive, there is a radio. And you can count on those two dudes up there to keep the pressure on and scare the shit out of everyone."

I looked at the police chief. He was as white as the middle of the French flag that he represented. Still tied up to his bar, he watched the landscape flash by him with an astonished disbelief. It was all a bad dream; this was completely beyond him. It wasn't possible for him to be on an adventure like this. He was handcuffed on a train with a bunch of stinking, dangerous crazies. I didn't really know what he could be thinking. In any case, he didn't seem to be listening to the grumbling of certain people who at last were beginning to balk. These were the kind who are never happy. It's only to be expected, it's a kind of lifestyle. They were saying things like: "The countryside is boring," "Only in Paris can you get a decent bite to eat," "Go begging around the cows, yeah right," "Gendarmes are stupid," "It's getting too sunny," "There's no metro down south." Some guys were regretting the trip; they felt almost homesick already. They started believing

Outside, everything was becoming more and more green and gold.
The suburbs had petered out. There were fields, small villages, steeples.

that, farther on, it was going to be hell, because they were likely to find people there even poorer and more helpless than themselves.

Outside, everything was becoming more and more green and gold. The suburbs had petered out. There were fields, small villages, steeples.

The platforms of the station at Dourdan were full of people who had come to see the phantom train go by. They were the curious. I saw some cameras. All of France knew about our train and wanted front row seats; we weren't going to pass by unnoticed. They shouted as we went by, some waved, but most gaped. So, this train really did exist. It wasn't just a joke.

Aboard, some people were getting sick. The bad wine had led to violent puking. The police chief himself had taken a good hit of purple splatter on his shoes and was on the edge of collapse.

Those who were not sick, those who were not plunged in comatose sleep, started complaining. They wanted water, they wondered what they were going to eat, and they looked for other reasons to be unhappy. My uncle shouted at them, calling them sheep-brained losers, and harshly advised them to figure out what they wanted, once and for all. They were going to see the ocean—shit, what did they have to complain about?

My uncle seemed to be growing younger. I no longer noticed his seventy years. He belched, pitching along the corridors, sometimes dropping down onto a seat, his face profoundly flushed but with an Olympic glow.

And then the train slowed and stopped in the middle of the countryside.

Some of the Makhnos got out immediately, in order to meet up with those in the locomotive. My uncle also jumped out onto the gravel. Through the window I heard them discussing things, just below me. Everything was fine. The Railway, for the moment, had opened the track, on the condition that we didn't go faster than forty-five miles per hour. They wanted us to stop at the station in Aubrais in order to renegotiate. The Draft Dodger, speaking for our group, had accepted this on the condition that our side could take advantage of situation to have supplies brought to us, something to drink and eat. Then we would see. Over the radio, numerous people had tried, with serious words and voices, to ask us to be more or less reasonable, that this couldn't go on forever, that there would be no repression or lawsuit started, but that we had to stop, that the distance already travelled was really far enough, that we had proved our case, that now we were front cover news, that we should be happy, that the homeless had had their trench-battle, but that this was now something unmanageable, that it was dangerous, all this. They contradicted themselves, not knowing how to put forward a package neatly tied up with threats, paternalism, and panic. Someone might fall off the train and we would be responsible—they had warned us.

My uncle was laughing at least as much as the Makhnos.

A first negotiation had already taken place and had concluded with no progress. It was out of the question for the Railway to let us travel on the southeast train line; there was too much traffic, it was too dangerous, too complicated, and not all of the secondary lines were electrified.

"There's no question of us backing down," the anarchists retorted. "We're going to see the great, blue ocean."

The other side had a counter proposal that would allow us to see the sea: to let us go on to Sète. This offer was accepted.

To go to the hometown of Georges Brassens, the anarchist musician—that was fair, my uncle judged.

But that was when a bunch of guys jumped off the train, and some began to run like rabbits into the nearby fields. My uncle was shouting after them, trying to get them to stop, but it didn't do any good. They were running away from a nightmare that they had decided they couldn't handle. Our five train cars were now half empty.

Wounded to the core, the anarchist leaders nevertheless decided that no one would be forced to continue. This wasn't Kronstadt. Everyone was asked to choose, and we did the sorting. We got rid of everyone who didn't want to continue— many of them didn't even know why. Inside the thick fog of their drunkenness, they no longer knew where they were. A few were crying, begging for the shouting and arguing to stop. It was necessary to carry some to the bottom of the footrail. There was some sweettalking, some grandiose speechmaking about cowardice, and some radical injunctions to go get screwed.

I was tempted for a brief moment to leave then, too, and do what I could on my own to get back home. It wasn't out of fear, but simply because everything was so green around us, and those quiet fields bordered by rustling trees suddenly seemed to me to be the most calm, restful, beautiful place.

But I was starting to care more and more about my uncle's respect. Despite his rags, despite his drunkard's face, I gradually understood the hostile and unfair ways in which our family had treated him. He was a real desperado, the kind of guy who did not live well except under galloping entropy. I was beginning to understand why he had given up on everything in order to slowly commit suicide beside the gutters in the Place de Vosges. He couldn't help himself. He knew that the family would never really understand his unhappiness. And now, through this grotesque and incredible adventure, he was gradually coming back to the world. He was doing it in opposition to the others, in opposition to the family, but not in opposition to me. It was *for* me, maybe. It was in order to leave me a small, positive image of him, something that I could keep for a long time in the wallet of my memory. I had to stay.

And then, once again, he distinguished himself. He remembered the mechanic in Buster Keaton's film *The General*, and persuaded us to detach the last train car, in order to avoid being pursued. We did it quickly.

Then we set off again. The engine groaned, as did the train cars. We watched as, at the end of a straight line of track, the lone train car we'd left behind disappeared, looking ridiculous and lost on the gleaming rails.

We made ourselves at home. We opened the doors and chucked out everything getting in the way. We cleaned house, leaving a real garbage dump alongside the tracks. From the back door we saw greasy papers and pieces of cardboard flying, we saw the glittering shards of numerous broken bottles.

"It's all biodegradable!" shouted my uncle. "Just like us!"

We divided ourselves up. From now on everyone had their own compartment assigned. Then, we divvied up the supplies. We collected everything that could serve as a projectile, we brought together the rest of the food, and all of the wine. We made plans. The trip became organized. Our surroundings became almost acceptable. We were going to leave this place in the state in which we had found it—well, almost. This train was, however, a sort of scenic railway for the broke, from the blocked johns to the half-gutted seats, with a strange group of clandestine passengers. There were about forty disheveled tramps, with weeping eyes and filth getting the upper hand, and a dozen madmen in leather who thought they were the Jesse James gang riding on the Pony Express.

Everyone sat down in their compartments, letting themselves be gently rocked by the regular rhythm of the rails. A few look-outs stayed at the windows to keep an eye on the roads, bridges, and stations, and to try to spot any pursuit or tail on us. At smaller stations, there was sometimes a crowd that waved to us. The engine often whistled. It now felt like a kind of traveling summer camp.

For a while, before we reached Orleans, my eyes followed the long, unfinished concrete track meant for the aerotrain. It ran alongside our track for fifteen miles or so, a completely useless thing. I couldn't help but think about all the dough that had been invested in that dead-end project, money that could have supported the occupants of our train for the rest of their lives.

The train slowly rumbled over the switches at the Aubrais station. Each time our train passed a switch, my heart was in my throat. At low speed, the Railway could have derailed us, immobilizing us forever. They had steered us onto one of the last tracks. We noticed a lively crowd around the station. There were also a lot of cops, and the riot squad must have been guarding all the entrances and exits.

When the train came to a stop, a heavy silence fell over us.

We were all at the windows, watching the movements of the crowd, three platforms away.

A small electric cart with three trailers hooked up to it drove along the platform to meet us. It stopped beside us and the driver immediately left on foot, going back towards the station.

"Those pigs," grumbled my uncle, "they've only given us water!"

Sure enough, there were several bundles of Evian bottles on the little carts. Nothing to burn our brains—safety precautions. The detox program was already starting, long distance. Two anarchists jumped out to load the stuff onto the train. There were also some of the usual French National Railway sandwiches, in their crackly plastic wrap.

"Check the expiration date," Guy muttered. "They might be trying to poison us!"

"It's paté," replied one of the guys on the platform.

"Be careful!" One of the anarchists from the engine started shouting, pointing to a small group of men in dark blue spilling out like magic from a stairwell in the middle of the platform. They were the SWAT team or some shit like that. One of the anarchists who had been loading the water jumped up on the foot-rail and fired two shots in their direction, aiming above their heads.

"Go back or we'll shoot the police chief," shouted my uncle.

The police athletes immediately disappeared down the stairway. We returned to an impasse. That must have been a fucking setback for them, and it was for us, too. At this rate, the police chief wouldn't last much longer.

At my window, I was breaking out in a cold sweat and had started trembling.

This was a fucking mess. Once considered the buddies of the respected Abbé Pierre, now we had become die-hard terrorists. Stealthily, we had been pushed down a slippery slope with no escape route. We would be hunted down like rabbits. Things were looking grim. The Special Forces were not far away, and probably helicopters, snipers, all that stuff; they were just waiting to put a bullet in your head while you slept.

I wasn't the only one thinking this way, because about ten loud-mouth tramps and three nervous younger guys chose that moment to jump off the train and run towards the station across the tracks.

"You bunch of idiots!" my uncle shouted, "They'll slaughter you! You'll pay for all of us! Fools!"

In front of us the signal was still red—we couldn't start off yet. It felt like something was getting ready to happen. At my feet, a guy was snoring heavily. When he woke up, it would take him a while to understand the shit he was in, far from Paris, an outlaw on the front line.

We stayed there for a long moment. Then a strange thought ran through my mind. I no longer felt afraid and I no longer wanted to leave, to get away. I only wanted one thing: that this would be over. It didn't matter how. I was practically sure that whatever happened would be in some sense a liberation, something which I would be able to claim for myself for a long time to come. It would be my own valorous deed, my own 1968. My battle. I had been there, not you.

Then another guy showed up, all alone. He was a station master or something like that, wearing a cap with four stars. He was a train general, at least.

We let him come all the way to us.

"This is getting to be some kind of joke, guys," he said, out of breath.

"Who's joking?" replied our spokesman, the Draft Dodger. "All that we want is to get to the sea. Then we'll surrender."

"But that's stupid!"

"It's not stupid, it's vital."

He took off his cap to wipe his large forehead.

"Just come with us," said the Draft Dodger, laughing. "We'll pretend to take you hostage and you'll see the big blue sea, too."

"Right. Like I've got the fucking time for that. I've got 200 riot police on my back in the station, plus the SWAT team, plus my boss, plus two slicks from the Ministry of the Interior, and a shit-load of journalists."

"It'll be good advertising for the company."

"Don't laugh."

"We're not laughing."

The station master breathed loudly. "OK, here's the deal: they want you to release the police chief—it seems he has a heart problem—and take a doctor and a ministry official in his place. They're both volunteers."

"Tell them that heart trouble or no, the chief is gonna die if this track isn't clear in five minutes."

"But I can't just tell them that. I have to take them something."

The Draft Dodger, out of patience, started shouting. "That's their fucking problem. They were the ones who shot first, damn it! You just tell them that we'll stop at Vierzon. By the time we get there, we'll have thought about their proposition. You've got five minutes! No more!"

And then he fired a shot in the air. The guy with the cap took off running.

"Now he's really screwed, that station master," a tramp said, quoting a popular Brassens song.

Nobody laughed.

Two minutes later, the signal changed to green.

It started all over again, just like in '14.

We had a nice trip. It was an hour and a half of peaceful travel. Everyone was sprawling on the seats, with the warm breeze coming in the windows. The stench, little by little, was swept away by the wind and it became breathable in there. There weren't many people left in our train—barely thirty passengers, including three women. There were about twenty tramps, ten excited Makhnos, and the two hostages, who seemed not to be enjoying the trip, based on the completely panicked look of the police chief who was still attached to the window bar.

Spirits lifted a bit; we started believing in Sète. My uncle described the station, with its awning, just next to the port, where the boats lolled about. And these were not just any kind of boats—they were wine boats, those carrying the cheap Hérault wine to vinegar makers around the world. His audience was laughing. Some of them already had the desire to get on board one of those boats and dive into the wine tanks, leaving for faraway parts while swimming in red wine. It would be paradise!

A helicopter had been following us for a while, like a shit-fly. Since there might be cameras on board, the guys took turns making obscene gestures towards it, in order to keep up the pressure.

The problem at the moment was that there was only water on board. That was serious. Thank goodness for Vierzon.

The train stopped just underneath the big colored bridge, all the way at the end of the Vierzon station. The Makhnos had already negotiated by telephone with the authorities. There would be a trade: beer, lots of it, in exchange for one of the hostages. They had decided to unload the Railway official.

"You wanted to see Vierzon, well, you've seen Vierzon," laughed my uncle, quoting Jacques Brel.

He was of no use anymore, our train-boss, since the anarchists had figured out how this kind of machine operates. As a hostage, he wasn't much good, but his liberation for a palette of beer cans seemed like it would be another victory for us. The police chief could still serve amply as our shield.

From where we were, we couldn't see much of what was happening in the station. We could see some sort of a commotion and people in uniforms, but it didn't seem like anyone was going to try the same trick they'd attempted at Aubrais. They understood now that we were dangerous and determined. There was no hurry. As soon as the engineer set his foot on the asphalt of the platform, a tire cart filled with cases of six-packs started towards us, pulled by two guys in blue overalls.

What seemed strange to me was that there was no one on the bridge above us. It was such a pretty bridge, painted in psychedelic colors. They must have blocked access to avoid mobs of supporters. They didn't want a crowd coming to cheer us while eating grilled hot-dogs, since we must be the headline of every news story. Seeing something like this, live, was candy for the carrion-gobbling spectators. We'd already noticed it on the little radios we still had in the train. It was really ramping up: "The Tramps from Hell." "The Train Trip to Shame." "They have nothing to lose except their alcoholic delusions," etc. And, of course, saying that the police chief was a good father, with two young children.

While everyone was laughing and watching the cases of beer arrive, I couldn't take my eyes off the steel girders above us, which seemed like a mute menace, a foreboding image of brutality. Far away, on the station side, there was still the same silence.

"They're being very quiet, these pigs," belched my uncle. "It's almost as if they're full, like wild animals after feasting on the kill."

When the cart carrying the beer reached us, four guys got off the train to load everything on board the first car. They grabbed hold of the cases of six-packs and started throwing them into the corridor.

On the bridge, I saw some sort of Batman-like figure. I wanted to say something, but everything got stuck in my throat. And what would I have said? Look out? Death is above us? It was completely ridiculous.

My eyes were still glued up above when I heard the first beer can pop open.

Then the guy in a black body-suit jumped from the bridge.

All the rest happened very quickly. My hands never stopped clenching the window bar.

The batman landed on the roof of the third car, a wire in his hands. It was a cord of steel upon which were sliding, at high speed, a dozen more guys in ski masks, fucking flying spiders.

Not one sound came from my throat. My mouth was dry. My finger pointed at them.

The Draft Dodger spotted me, understood that something was wrong, and jumped off the train with his pistol in his hand. He too looking up in the air. I saw his chest jolt as if he was struck with an epileptic seizure and he fell backwards onto the middle of the tracks.

I never heard a single shot. The other armed anarchist, just like in the movies, fired two or three shots through the metal roof of the train car. But one of the assailants was already at the end of the car, with a strange, long weapon in his grasp. I

It was a cord of steel upon which were sliding, at high speed,
a dozen more guys in ski masks, fucking flying spiders.

saw the head of the Makhno disappear as if by magic. There was a pink cloud around him.

I threw myself on the ground. Everything went white as if there was ether in the air.

I guess that my uncle had jumped on one of the pistols that had fallen on the ground and was brandishing it and shouting. And then he disappeared, falling back under the impact of bullets, into the compartment from which he had emerged.

I just had time, before screaming, to see a huge black spider jump on me, flip me over like a pancake, and crush my nose into the floor, warning me not to move a muscle, not a single muscle.

I heard the crackle of a walkie-talkie.

Then a voice, calm, poised, and cold: "Mission terminated. All secure."

About the Author

Jean-Bernard Pouy was born on January 2, 1946 in Nérac, a town in Aquitaine, southwestern France, but grew up in Paris. After earning a DEA degree in Art History, focusing on Cinema, he worked as a high-school counselor in Paris from 1972-80. He has also worked as a drawing teacher, graphic designer, proofreader, and scriptwriter, and sometimes went without work. His first novel, *Spinoza Encule Hegel* (1983), took an ironic view of the revolutionary atmosphere of Paris in 1968: an armed and suicidal band of ten Spinozists enter a confrontation with the Hegelians.

Pouy's best-known creation is the distinctly anarchistic fictional character Gabriel Lecouvreur, who is called Le Poulpe (meaning "the octopus," but also a play on words evoking pulp fiction), who has appeared in a series of popular stories. The most important innovation of the Le Poulpe series is to use the detective story as a tool of contemporary social critique and resistance. This series has included a number of collaborative efforts, including titles co-authored by Pouy and other writers, a title written by a group of high school students, and one created by a network of bloggers. The Cheryl series has spun off from Le Poulpe, featuring Lecouvreur's girlfriend Cheryl as the main protagonist.

Full Fare is the first English translation of anything Pouy has written. This is partly due to the prevalence of contemporary slang and the distinctly French settings in Pouy's writing. The translation and editing of this work have been major undertakings, but it is hoped that this will be a first taste for English-language readers of what Francophone readers have been enjoying for years.